FIESTA FIASCO

by **ANN WHITFORD PAUL**

illustrated by **ETHAN LONG**

Holiday House / New York

For Rob and Alma
Muchas Gracias
A. W. P.
For Linda and Emmett
E. L.

Text copyright © 2007 by Ann Whitford Paul
Illustrations copyright © 2007 by Ethan Long
All Rights Reserved
Printed and Bound in 9/09 at Kwong Fat Offset Printing, Ltd.,
Dongguan City, Guangdong Province, China.
The text typeface is Barcelona.
The artwork was created with gouache and colored pencil.
www.holidayhouse.com

3 5 7 9 10 8 6 4 2

Library of Congress Cataloging-in-Publication Data
Paul, Ann Whitford.
Fiesta fiasco / by Ann Whitford Paul ; illustrated by Ethan Long. — 1st ed.
p. cm.
Summary: When shopping for Culebra's birthday, Conejo convinces his friends Iguana and Tortuga
to buy all the wrong presents. Includes a glossary of Spanish words used.
ISBN-13: 978-0-8234-2037-7 (hardcover)
ISBN-13: 978-0-8234-2275-3 (paperback)
(1. Rabbits—Fiction. 2. Desert animals—Fiction. 3. Gifts—Fiction.) I. Long, Ethan, ill. II. Title.
PZ7.P278338Fi 2007
(E)—dc22
2006012112

GLOSSARY

Clothing

camisa	cah-MEE-sah	shirt
pantalones	pahn-tah-LOW-nehs	pants
sombrero	some-BRAY-roh	hat

Other words in Spanish

conejo	co-NAY-ho	rabbit
culebra	cu-LAY-brah	snake
cumpleaños	coom-pleh-AH-nyohs	birthday
feliz	fay-LEES	happy
fiesta	fee-EST-ah	party
globo	GLOW-boh	balloon
libro	LEE-broh	book
regalo(s)	ray-GAH-low(s)	gift(s)
tazón	tah-SOHN	bowl
torta	TORE-tah	cake
tortuga	tor-TU-gah	tortoise

Conejo hopped over to Iguana.
"I'm going to the market to buy
a *regalo* for Culebra's *cumpleaños*."
"I need to buy Culebra a birthday gift, too,"
said Iguana.
Tortuga peered out of his shell. "So do I."

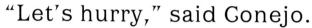

"Let's hurry," said Conejo.
"His *fiesta* starts soon."
"We can't be late for his party,"
said Iguana.

At the market vendors
were selling bananas and
tomatoes, tacos
and tortillas,
jewelry and shawls—
all sorts of things.

"A *globo*!" said Iguana.
"Culebra would love
a balloon."
Conejo laughed.
"What good is a *globo*?
Get him that *sombrero*.
A hat will keep
the sun off his head."

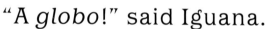

"Why don't *you* buy him
    the *sombrero*?" asked Iguana.
He glared at her.
"I have another gift in mind.
    Besides, I'm an expert
    at choosing gifts.
    Buy him that *sombrero*."
And Iguana did.

"I'll give Culebra this *tazón*," said Tortuga.

Conejo snickered.
"Culebra doesn't need a bowl.
He needs a *camisa*."
"Why does he need a shirt?"
asked Tortuga.
"Doesn't Culebra always say he'll grow
arms?" asked Conejo.
Tortuga nodded. "Whenever
he wants to get out of work."
"See!" Conejo held his head high.
"Buy him a *camisa*."
So Tortuga did.

"Now I need my *regalo* for Culebra," said Conejo.
"What about a *libro*?" asked Iguana.
"Culebra loves a good book," added Tortuga.

"Culebra doesn't want a *libro*,"
cried Conejo. "He wants *pantalones*."
"Stop!" said Iguana.
"Culebra doesn't want pants,"
said Tortuga. "He has no legs."
"But when Culebra grows arms,
he'll grow legs, too,"
said Conejo.

Conejo pounded his chest.
"I know best.
I will buy Culebra *pantalones*."
And Conejo did.

Back at Iguana's they had just finished wrapping their *regalos* when Culebra arrived for the *fiesta*.

"Let's play games," said Iguana.
"No!" said Conejo. "Culebra should open his *regalos.*"
"Before we sing '*Feliz Cumpleaños*' and eat *torta*?"
asked Tortuga.
"'Happy Birthday' and cake can wait." Conejo shoved
Iguana's *regalo* at Culebra. "Open it *now.*"

Culebra tore open the box.
He stared.
"It's a *sombrero*," Conejo explained.
"I know what it is," said Culebra.
"What am I supposed to do with it?"
"Wear it to keep the sun away,"
said Conejo.
"But I like the sun," said Culebra.

Conejo grabbed
the *sombrero*.
"Then I'll wear it."

Next Culebra opened Tortuga's *regalo*. "A *camisa*?" "You'll need it when you grow arms, but," Conejo said, "until then . . ."

Conejo put on the *camisa* and handed
Culebra his *regalo*.

"I'm afraid to open this."
Culebra untied the ribbon.
He looked inside. "*Pantalones*?"
"For when you grow legs,"
said Conejo.

Conejo put on the *pantalones*.
Iguana, Tortuga, and Culebra stared
at Conejo, all dressed up in Culebra's
sombrero, *camisa*, and *pantalones*.
"You tricked us!" shouted Iguana.
"Why did we listen to you?" asked Tortuga.

"You picked out my presents for yourself," said Culebra. "Go away!"

"But we haven't played games,"
said Conejo. "We haven't
eaten *torta*."
Culebra shook his rattle.
"I don't want you at my *fiesta*."
Conejo's head hung low.
Off he slumped.

Iguana, Tortuga, and
Culebra played
Pin the Tail
on the Coyote.

They played Cactus,
the desert game of Statues.

And they played Musical Rocks.
Just then Conejo came back.
"Go away," said Iguana.
"Culebra doesn't want you here," added Tortuga.
"Wait!" said Culebra. "You took off the clothes."
"I returned them."

"Then what's in your bag?" asked Culebra.
"Here," Conejo said.
"This *regalo* is from Iguana."
"A *globo*!" said Culebra.
"I love this. It's my favorite color!"

"This *regalo* is from Tortuga."
"A *tazón*!" exclaimed Culebra.
"Now I won't have to eat off
a rock anymore."
Then Conejo handed
him a *libro*. "This is from me.
But it was Tortuga and
Iguana's idea."
"I've been wanting to read
this," said Culebra.
"Thank you."

Then they all sang "*Feliz Cumpleaños.*"

Iguana served the *torta*.
"I love *cumpleaños*!"
Tortuga said. "Whose is next?"
"My *cumpleaños*!" Conejo
hopped up and down.
"Mine is next."

Culebra laughed. "Your *cumpleaños* will be easy."

Conejo wrinkled his brow. "Why?"

"Because," said Iguana, "we all know what *regalos* to buy *you*."

And they did.